The Amazing Adventures of Superfeet

The Amazing Adventures of Superfeet
The Awesome Book

Lynda Sturdevant

READERSMAGNET, LLC

The Amazing Adventures of Superfeet
Copyright © 2018 by Lynda Sturdevant

Published in the United States of America
ISBN Paperback: 978-1-947765-90-0
ISBN eBook: 978-1-947765-91-7

All rights reserved. No part of this publication may be reproduced, stored in a retrieval system or transmitted in any way by any means, electronic, mechanical, photocopy, recording or otherwise without the prior permission of the author except as provided by USA copyright law.

The opinions expressed by the author are not necessarily those of ReadersMagnet, LLC.

ReadersMagnet, LLC
10620 Treena Street, Suite 230 | San Diego, California, 92131 USA
1.619.354.2643 | www.readersmagnet.com

Book design copyright © 2018 by ReadersMagnet, LLC. All rights reserved.
Cover design by Ericka Walker
Interior design by Shieldon Watson

Dedication

Dedicated to the memory of my beloved son, Jared Sturdevant and his loving fiancé Ashkea Wood—our perfect angels.

Acknowledgements

I would like to express my appreciation to my family and friends who are a source of encouragement, support, and inspiration.

I would also like to give a special thank you to my grandson, Chance, and nephew, Sam for their youthful insight.

For her friendship and assistance, which proved invaluable to me, I am deeply grateful to Jennifer N. Young.

Table of Contents

Prologue 11
The Land Of All 13
It's a Great Day 19
The Stranger 31
Grace's Healing 36
The Coming Storm 40
Vivian Believes 44
God's Armor 49
Ben's Revelation 55
To The Rescue 61
The Mystery of the Tower 66
Grandpa's Treasure 76
Afterword 81
Bibliography 83

Prologue

Though Grandpa Gideon is now in heaven, his legacy would continue on. Especially in the heart and mind of his cherished granddaughter, Lacy, whom he had left his *Awesome Book* to. The power of his influence and the books might would soon be evident to all those he loved.

The Land Of All

Lacy raised her arms to embrace God and was filled with His presence. Being lifted from the earth she was now flying and the wind was under her feet. She ascended high into the heavens so fast it tickled her tummy. Up and over lush green valleys dotted with trees and flowing streams, which glistened in the dawning light, soaring higher and higher until she finally came to a lofty mountain ridge. As she descended, Lacy became aware that she was no longer wearing her pajamas, but a shining, white tunic cinched at the waist and tied in a bow on the left side. On her feet were tall red boots with red shoelaces, just like the one she used as a bookmark.

Lacy marveled at what she had experienced at the beauty of her surroundings. Her eyes drank in the vibrant hues of the rainbow that hung in the mist that blanketed the valley below. Lots of questions flooded her mind, but her thoughts were interrupted by the faint sound of crying. It was a cry for help.

"Lacy, you must go and help," whispered Holy Spirit.

"How will I know what to do?" she asked.

"I have a plan. I have given you gifts that will help you in all you do for God. I will never leave you. And, in answer to your questions, without the white clothing and red boots, you could not travel on the wind of the Spirit. All you have need of is provided for you in the kingdom of God if you seek God first and his righteousness. It is the land of 'All,' where God is all and in all and where all things are possible."

"Thank you for helping me understand."

"I have many treasures for you to find," said Holy Spirit. "Let us go now."

Lacy lifted her hands and embraced the Lord; leaving behind the magenta and violet mountain peaks, she flew swiftly upon the Spirit's wind to where she heard the cry. Standing in a back yard, with hands over her eyes, was a woman weeping and praying. She was unaware of Lacy descending a few feet in front of her.

"Can I do something to help?" questioned Lacy.

The woman, looking up, was startled to see Lacy there. Knowing there was no one there a few seconds ago, she thought she was seeing an angel.

"Are you an angel?" asked the woman.

"No. I'm just a girl. I heard you cry from the mountain ridge and Holy Spirit told me I needed to come and help. He said he would show me how."

"From the mountain ridge? What mountain ridge? How did you get there? I'm sorry; did you say the Holy Spirit sent you?"

"Yes. He really did." said Lacy. "He brought me here on the wind. What can I do to help?"

The woman just stood there, eyes gaping with a bewildered look on her face. Finally, she sputtered, "But you're just a child!" After a long pause she added, "Please forgive me, I guess I just wasn't expecting God to answer my prayer in this manner, although, I know God works in mysterious ways."

"My name is Grace, and I cannot find my son Soul. Though I warned and forbade him, he took the road called Disobedience and has not been able find his way home. I prayed God would send someone to help. But you cannot go down that road," she said. "For it is filled with pitfalls."

"Don't worry," said Lacy. "God is is with me. We will find him."

Once again, Lacy raised her hands to heaven and was lifted above the countryside, with the wind under her feet. From there she could see for miles and miles. She saw the crossroads where Soul must have turned down Disobedience Road.

The road disappeared into the thick foreboding darkness of an immense forest. The land was gloomy and dreary; colorless. Even the trees were black, gnarled, withered and twisted. She traveled on the wind for miles not knowing what direction the road may have turned. Her eyes searched diligently, and she listened for any instructions. Then she prayed, *God, show me where he is, please.*

"Just over the next hill," whispered the Holy Spirit.

As she flew over the top of the hill a light shined from heaven into the darkness of the forest and the road came back into view. Although wide, it abruptly ended at a dark murky pool surrounded by trees with huge thorns and dense briary underbush.

"There he is!" she cried out.

And there he certainly was, stuck in a pool of muck. He struggled and struggled to get out, but only sunk further. He was all worn out and about to go under when Lacy swooped down, just in nick of time, and grabbed his arm. It surprised her how easy it was to pull him out. She carried him to the side of the pool and dropped him with a bit of a thud.

"Ouch!" he groaned.

"Sorry about that," said Lacy slinging muck from her hand, "You're my first."

"I guess I should thank you." said Soul. "I almost drowned in that pool of muck.

"How did you get in there?" Lacy asked.

Soul replied, "I got lost following this old road. It got so dark that I couldn't see. That's when I stubbed my big toe on a rock and jammed it. I stumbled and fell into the pool of muck and couldn't get out. And, well, you know the rest of the story."

"Yeah, you were stuck in the muck all right!"

They both laughed because Soul was covered with gunk from head to toe, and he sure smelled bad too!

Soul suddenly realized a miracle had just taken place and asked, "You're an angel aren't you?"

"No," said Lacy. "I'm just a girl who believes in Jesus."

"How come you can fly then? And how come you're dressed weird? And why are you so strong?"

"I didn't, I mean. I wasn't until this morning," replied Lacy.

So Lacy introduced herself and told Soul everything that happened to her regarding *The Awesome Book* with its powerful words, the wind and the light, and how she met Jesus, Father, and Holy Spirit.

"I bet God would live in you too, if you would just believe," she said.

"My mom talks about that stuff all the time," said Soul.

"You have heard about the words of *The Awesome Book* too?"

"Oh yeah," he answered. "But I didn't think it was true until now. When I got stuck in the muck and couldn't get out, I got real scared. I prayed that God would help me, and uh, well, anyway, I appreciate what you did for me."

"I was happy to help. We had better get you home."

Holy Spirit whispered to Soul, "Take hold of Lacy's hand."

When Lacy lifted up her arms to heaven, she and Soul began to rise.

Soul believed in Jesus that day and was cleansed from the muck. He was safely carried by the wind back to his home.

Lacy said goodbye and the wind lifted her up again and she disappeared out of sight.

Anticipating his return after her divine encounter, Soul's mother was making breakfast for him when the door flung open and he ran in. Catching his toe on the rug, he tumbled headlong over the footstool, and went sprawling out on the floor. He scrambled to his feet and began hopping around on his left foot while holding the big toe of the other. As he hopped he cried, "Mother, please forgive me for running away. I know that Disobedience is definitely the wrong road to take. It only leads you to the pool of muck."

This confession was a comical sight, but Grace did not allow herself to laugh.

"Didn't I tell you, this is how *The Awesome Book* said it would be son?"

"Yeah, I know Mom, and you were so right. I was in a lot of trouble, stuck in that gunk until, uh, until, oh you wouldn't believe it!"

"Until the girl in the shiny white clothes with the super feet came to help?"

"Yeah, Mom, you're really good!"

She just smiled and sat down at the table. There would be much to talk about over breakfast. They gave thanks to God for their daily bread, for the girl Grace fondly called Superfeet, and for a lesson well learned.

It's a Great Day

Lacy awoke and saw Grandpa's *Awesome Book* lying on the bed next to her.

Delighted, Lacy thought, *That dream about Grace and Soul seemed so real. It would be wonderful to really be able to fly and rescue people in trouble. Like a superhero!*

"Superfeeeet!" She sang to the tune of Superman.

"Ha!" She laughed at herself for thinking such things.

Sitting on the edge of her bed, she looked up to Heaven and said, "Good morning Heavenly Father. Thank you for *The Awesome Book.*"

There was silence for what Lacy thought to be a long time, but she waited patiently, believing she would not be disappointed. Breaking the silence she heard Holy Spirit say, "Jesus '...sent them two by two...'" (Luke 10:1 NKJV)

"What do you mean?" Lacy asked.

"Luke, chapter 10," whispered Holy Spirit.

It wasn't long before she found the place. She read each verse very carefully.

It was amazing what Jesus' disciples could do. Jesus gave them power to heal people of diseases, just like he did. Even devils had to obey when they used his name.

Looking again at the book she read aloud, "Notwithstanding in this rejoice not, that the spirits are subject unto you; but rather rejoice, because your names are written in heaven." (Luke 10:20 KJV)

"Lacy, time to get up." her mother called. "Breakfast is almost ready. Wash up and get dressed."

"Sorry God, I have to go now. Thank you so much for writing my name in your book and revealing your wisdom to me." After putting the red shoelace back she carefully closed *The Awesome Book* and laid it on the table by her bed. Lacy quickly dressed and washed her face. Brushing her fiery red locks back into a short, untidy ponytail, she smiled at herself in the mirror, thinking, *If I felt any happier, I could almost smile ear to ear.* She closed her eyes and imagined her lips stretching across her face until they touched her ears.

Her mother, Gloria, had come in and was standing in the doorway of the bathroom watching Lacy's face through the mirror; it astounded her how much her daughter's face looked like her own.

"Are you daydreaming again, Lacy?"

Lacy opened her big emerald eyes and giggled.

"Well…I was just thinking how funny it would be if I could smile from ear to ear." she responded, giggling again.

"Oh Lacy, the things you come up with!"

Gloria was amused at her daughter's sense of humor. She closed her eyes and imagined smiling until her lips were touching her ears also, and with a big smile she said, "That would be funny Lacy. You sure remind me of myself when I was your age."

"Really? I do?" asked Lacy happily.

"Yes, you really do. Come on, let's go."

Breakfast was on the table and smelled so good. Pancakes, just the way Lacy loved them, with blueberries and whipped topping.

"This looks great Mom, thanks."

Lacy's baby brother, Todd, was sitting in his high chair next to her dad. His little, inquisitive, blue eyes lit up at the sight of his big sister. Lacy sat down in the chair next to him and kissed his forehead, then tousled his matching fiery red locks with her fingers.

"It's a great day little guy, a great day." she said.

"Well, just listen to you. What has brought on all this great day stuff?" inquired Dad.

"I was just reading Grandpa's *Awesome Book*. Did you know that God writes his disciples names down in heaven?"

Her father wondered what she was talking about, but he just smiled.

Gloria set a glass of milk on the table before Lacy and sat down, then ask, "Who wants to say grace?" "Oh, let me say it today," requested Lacy.

"Of course you may Lacy," said Dad.

"Thank you for everything and bless this food and Mom for preparing it. Bless Dad and little Todd. Thank you for my family. Amen."

"Well I think that was very nice Lacy," Mom expressed proudly.

"Eat up Lacy, and don't dawdle," remarked Dad. "We have plans to drive to the country after breakfast and visit the Thompson's."

Suddenly, the day didn't seem quite so great.

"The Thompon's, for all day long?" Lacy whined.

"It will be all right Lacy, you will still have a great day," said Mom.

"But I wanted to go to Shelly's house and ride horses today. Her dad bought a new horse and she asked me to come riding with her. It's dapple gray just like the one I always dreamed about and she said I could ride it. Pleeeease Mom? I can go to the Thompson's some other time. Besides, Rachael isn't there and I don't want to go if she's not there. It'll be boring. And I already told Shelly I would."

"Well, for one thing young lady, you didn't ask to go to Shelly's. And if this is a new horse, we don't know how trained it is. Maybe you can go riding with Shelly next week, but first we need to speak with her father about the horse. It's been a couple of months since we've seen Ben and Vivian. I know they would be disappointed if you didn't come.

"Please Mom?"

"I'm sorry Lacy, but I insist you go with us.

"But Mom!"

"No buts, and that's final. Now stop your whining and eat your breakfast.

Then afterward, call Shelly and tell her you can't come today."

"Daaad?"

"Lacy, your mother is right. Stop arguing with her. You're going with us and I don't want to hear any more about it!"

Lacy folded her arms and sat there with a big pout on her lips pleading with her eyes.

"That's not going to work," said Dad, "Now call Shelly and tell her you can't come. We'll be leaving after breakfast. And another thing."

"What?" Lacy smartly replied, before Frank finished his sentence.

"Apologize to your mother and change your attitude!" You know you have to ask before you make plans. Don't just presume that you'll be able to go somewhere until you clear it with us first." Is that understood?"

"Yes, Daddy," replied Lacy with a softer tone, then she returned to her mother said, "I'm sorry Mom."

Gloria gave her a big hug and said, "I love you Lacy."

Hugging her back, Lacy replied sorrowfully, "I love you too, Momma." Then she asked, "Is it okay if I take *The Awesome Book*?"

"it's a big worn, so you will have to be very careful with it."

"I will. Thank you Mom. It will give me something to do," she said with a sigh.

As they traveled, Lacy only looked up from *The Awesome Book* when someone pointed out something interesting along the way. She read all about Jesus's miraculous birth, his baptism, and how he had the power to heal, to cast out evil spirits and even raise the dead. She saw how Jesus loved and healed people, even those that nobody else cared about. *Jesus is a miracle* she thought to herself. *He is the Son of God in a man's body.* Lacy closed her eyes and embraced the warmth of Holy Spirit as she thought about her wonderful Jesus, and how he loved everyone so much. She was so peaceful with God all around her. She felt that everyone in the car must feel Him because He was there with her, in her, surrounding her and filling her with love.

"With *his* sweet *love!*"

Gloria looked over her shoulder at her children in the back seat who appeared to be sleeping peacefully. Light was emanating from Lacy's face causing it to glow.

"Odd," she said in a soft voice, "Must be the light filtering through the windows, what else could it be?"

Frank glanced at his wife with a troubled look, as if he wanted to say something, but instead he remained silent.

He reached over and turned on the radio. Gloria smiled, leaned back in her seat, and seemed content to just listen to the oldies and enjoy the drive.

At last the car pulled onto a long narrow drive, lined with huge oak trees on both sides. Nestled against a backdrop of the tall oaks and sycamores, at the end of the drive, was a very large, white, two story house with a covered porch that wrapped all the way around it. Although it needed a fresh coat of paint, it was still a beautiful old house. The back overlooked a steep hill with a small trail that disappeared into the shadows of the trees.

Lacy loved to explore the attic, which was complete with huge mirrors and trunks with treasures inside. When she was younger, the Thompson's daughter, Rachael, would play with her there. They would sit at the little wooden table and have a tea party with Rachael's dolls. Mrs. Thompson still allowed her to play in the attic and dress up in the clothing she kept stored in the trunks. Pretending she was a beautiful princess held captive, Lacy would cross the landing to the tower and look out the tower's main window, waiting for her knight in shining armor to rescue her from the evil emperor's castle.

However, after her last excursion there, she wasn't ready to go into the house yet. Instead, she went immediately to the swing that hung from the biggest tree in the yard and sat down. She was holding the big *Awesome Book* in her lap.

"I won't go in the attic this time, just in case it was real," she said to herself aloud.

"Just in case what is real?" came a voice from behind her.

Lacy let out a shriek and fell backward out of the swing clutching tightly to the big, black book.

"Don't you know not to sneak up on somebody like that!: she pouted.

"I'm sorry," said the boy as he reached out his hand to help Lacy to her feet.

Taking his hand, Lacy looked up and neither one could believe their eyes.

"It's you!" they both cried at the same time.

"You are Soul!"

"You are Lacy!"

"Wow, I can't believe this," exclaimed Lacy. "I thought it was all a dream. But you are real, or are you?"

Lacy reached out and pinched Soul on his arm.

"Ouch! That hurt. What are you doing?"

"I just wanted to make sure you wasn't a ghost."

"A ghost?"

"Yeah, I'm sorry," Lacy said. "Does it still hurt?"

"No. Not so much now," responded Soul as he rubbed his left arm.

"I was hoping I would see you again. Thanks again for getting me out of the pool of muck. You know," he said with a chuckle, "My mom thinks that you're an angel or maybe one of God's superheroes. She calls you Superfeet!"

Now that it was daylight and he wasn't covered in muck, Lacy could see his brilliant white hair and pale complexion, contrasting with his soft, chestnut eyes.

"It was just a dream," said Lacy.

"Do I look like a dream to you?" Soul asked with a big grin.

"No," said Lacy rather shyly, and then pinched herself.

"Owww!" she cried.

"Why did you do that?"

"I'm checking to see if I'm really awake."

Soul just laughed and asked, "You don't know when you're awake? Do ya space out a lot?"

Lacy just glared at him. He let it go and inquired, "You wanna go exploring?"

"Okay sounds like fun. But first, I need to put *The Awesome Book* in the house. Come with me while I ask my mom and dad if it's all right."

"Mom, Dad, this is my new friend, Soul, and we're going exploring, that is, if it's all right with you?"

Vivian Thompson spoke up. "I'm sure Lacy will be fine Frank. Soul lives down the road a little ways. His mother is a good friend of mine, and a fine Christian woman."

"Well then," said Lacy's father, "You two have a good time and be careful."

"I'll fix them up some lunch so they can have a picnic," said Vivian. She, Gloria and the kids then headed for the kitchen. "You knew that Rachael went to Europe to attend college," she continued, "Well she met a nice young man named Adam who is going to the Philippines with a group of young people to do missionary work. She has made arrangements to go too and work at an orphanage. I know that she's always had a love for, and a desire to work with children, but it still came as quite a surprise."

"Sounds like Adam has made quite an impression on her," said Gloria. "How long will she be in the Philippines?"

Vivian could not hide her concern. "It will only be for two weeks but of course we were looking forward to her coming home. We tried, but there was no talking her out of it. She's been attending worship services with him and now believes this is what God wants her to do." Then a faint smile crossed her face, "Yes, I think this dark haired; dark eyed Adam has made quite an impression. Anyway, it feels good to have some kids around. Things have been pretty quiet here since Rachael left, except for all the strange noises in the attic."

"Noises?" asked Gloria, "Maybe you have some pesky rodents?"

Vivian nodded her head and replied, "hmm probably," then busied herself with the task of making that picnic lunch.

Lacy didn't say anything but Mrs. Thompson's remark about the noise in the attic did not escape her attention.

Two kids departed down the steep, narrow pathway toward the Zoe River with their sack lunch in hand.

"Let's go down by the river and explore the old mill. We can have our picnic lunch there."

"I'm in," replied Lacy. "Lead the way."

They walked a short space down the long steep hill and disappeared into the woods. It didn't take them long to reach the valley below. As they were crossing the clearing, Lacy looked back, but could only see the top of the tower on the back of the old house. She was just glad she was down here with Soul instead of up there in that old, spooky tower.

The sun's rays felt good on Lacy's face, and in her heart she felt excited about the adventures ahead. Bursting with joy, she suddenly shouted, "What a great day!"

Soul was filled with joy and joined in. "What a great day!" they both shouted.

Lacy's dad had watched the pair until their heads bobbed out of sight. He stayed there a few minutes taking in the scenic view then turned to go inside. Just as his hand touched the door know the sound of great joy carried by the wind reached his ears and he began to laugh. When he entered the living room where everyone had gathered, he exclaimed loudly, "It's a great day!"

Suddenly everyone in the room was filled with the same joy and laughed too, including Ben Thompson, who was known to be pretty grumpy most of the time.

"It must be something in the air." he joked.

It's a great day they all agreed. Little

Todd laughed and clapped his hands together. "Gate day.", he said over and over, giggling after.

This got everyone laughing again.

The Stranger

Just across the clearing was the Zoe River and between the trees they could see the old mill. Vines had wrapped themselves around the mill, almost totally covering one side. They had also entangled themselves in the trees beside it.

"Looks kinda scary," said Lacy.

"Ah, there's nothing to be scared of," retorted Soul. "You'll see."

Finally, they reached the river and made their way down the bank toward the mill. Three huge bullfrogs were sunning themselves on the riverbank and leapt into the water when they got too close, while a small green lizard scurried ahead of them and found shelter under a rock.

Spying a big log Soul said, "Let's leave our lunch here on this big old log, then we ca eat after we explore the mill."

The trail ended at the riverside, so there was no path around the mill. The grass was so tall it was almost over their heads. Determined, Soul pressed on through the tall weeds blazing the trail with Lacy sticking close behind.

They were almost to the front of the mill when Soul looked back at Lacy, pulling his finger to his lips he whispered, "Shush."

Taking her hand, he pulled her down so they could not be seen in the tall grass.

"What is it?" whispered Lacy. "Is something wrong?"

"I saw someone." Soul said in a low whisper.

"Who was it?".

"Shush. I don't know. I hope its not that crazy old man."

"What crazy old man?" Questioned Lacy.

"I don't know. Just some old man. He's supposed to have gone crazy and then one they he just went missing. At least, that's what I heard."

"That's so sad," said Lacy. "If he just had God to help him."

"Hey! What are you young-uns doing here?" growled a gravelly, angry voice.

"Why are you hiding in the grass like a couple of snakes. You come out here right now so I can have a good look at you!.

Lacy and Soul stood up to face the stranger, who had snuck up on them.

"We're just ex-ex-exploring, mister." said Soul with a stutter.

Exploring, huh? Well, go explore someone else! The man growled again. "This is my home!"

"Lacy," whispered Holy Spirit, "This man's name is Jimmy, and I want you to tell him that God loves him."

Lacy was afraid to say anything and she stood there in silence quivering.

"Lacy," whispered Holy Spirit again a little louder, "Tell Jimmy God loves Him."

But Lacy was still frozen with fear and her mouth just refused to open. Then the crazy old man began yelling at them to get off his property or else.

Soul grabbed her arm to pull her away and with an anxious voice said. "Come on Lacy, let's go." "We've got to get out of here!"

Again, Holy Spirit spoke to Lacy, this time in a very serious tone, "Lacy, tell Jimmy that God loves him, now!"

Suddenly, Lacy's tongue was loose and she said with a loud voice, "Okay, I will!"

"You will what?" questioned the old man gruffly.

Lacy swallowed hard and silently prayed for courage.

"God wants me to tell you something." answered Lacy somewhat timidly.

"God?" Grumbled the old man, but not as loud.

Finally finding some boldness Lacy declared. "Yes, God. He said your name is Jimmy."

The old man looked shocked that Lacy knew his name. Since she went to heaven, his life had been terribly lonely. How he was also homeless, living in this old mill for shelter and felt that there was no hope left for him. His eyes filled with tears and with a soft voice he said, "What did God want you to tell me little lady?"

"That He loves you. God loves you, Jimmy."

Thank you, little girl, said the big, burly man as a big teardrop rolled down his stubbly cheek.

Not knowing what to say, Soul asked, "Would you like to share lunch with us?" We brought peanut butter and jelly sandwiches.

"I would love to," said Jim.

Though there were only two sandwiches, all three ate till they were full. There was even half a sandwich left over and one apple, which they left for Jim to eat later.

Lacy told Jim the whole story of *The Awesome Book* and her adventure with God. Then she told him about finding Soul up to his neck in the pool of muck, and how funny he looked after she pulled him out, "You couldn't even tell his hair was white at all! The only thing white was the white of his eyes peering through that sticky, smelly, greenish brown slime!"

They all had a great big laugh at Lacy's recollection.

"Man, it's been a lot of fun meeting you kids today. I haven't laughed like this in a long time. At least not since my dear sweet Jenny's been gone. Do you think the Lord would come and live in me if I asked Him to forgive me of my sins?" His hazel eyes widened, anticipating the answer.

"Of course," said Lacy.

"Of course," repeated Soul.

Jim grew very quiet and tilted his head slightly as if he was listening intently. Then he closed his eyes and moved his head up and down and began to groan lightly.

"I believe in Jesus. I believe!" Jim sobbed as he fell on his knees.

At that moment he was filled with the Holy Spirit and was set free from his sins and torment. When he stood up, his face was beaming with light, and he lifted his arms to heaven and shouted, "Thank you Lord, what a great day!"

"Wow," said Soul. "Now you're a Christian too!"

"I know God sent you kids here today for me," said Jim. Smiling, he added, "And for Jenny too."

"I didn't know we were being sent by God," said Soul.

"I did," remarked Lacy. "I did."

They spent the rest of the afternoon listening to Jim talked about the many adventures of his childhood. Soul laughed so hard one time that he fell off the log backward, tearing the seat of his pants. But he didn't get hurt, except for a bump on his head. Jim teased him about it being a good thing he landed on his noggin.

Soon it was time to go and the two explorers said goodbye and headed back up the trail toward the big, old, white house.

Grace's Healing

When they started back, Soul noticed it was about 4:00 pm. Excited about everything that had happened, they recapped play by play how God used them to help old Mr. Lee, who it turned out, wasn't so old after all. Lacy wondered if this is what it was like to be a disciple of God. She thought about Jim saying that God sent them to him and what she read in *The Awesome Book* about God sending His disciples out by twos. She shared her thoughts with Soul and told him she would show him the stories about Jesus' disciples and where it says God writes down their names in heaven.

"I didn't even know there was a book in heaven," said Soul. Holy Spirit whispered to Soul, "I will never leave you or forsake you my child."

Soul stopped dead in his tracks and closed his eyes and his heart was overcome with waves of love and peace. After a few moments he began to thank Heavenly Father for sending Jesus and Holy Spirit. He stood very still in God's presence, basking in His embrace, feeling the warmth of His light.

Lacy had walked on a short distance before realizing that she was walking alone and talking to herself. Turning around, she saw a brilliant light shining all around Soul. The wind of God's Spirit began to whirl around her and she lifted her arms in surrender and began to rise. She was joined by Soul and they were both filled with the light from the glory of God's presence, and the wind was beneath their feet. Both were dressed in shiny white tunics, except Soul, who also wore trousers that were a brilliant royal blue. The Glory Light reflected prisms of color throughout their clothing.

In an instant they were soaring above the Zoe River and saw their new friend Jim, still sitting on the big log where they had left him. He appeared to be praying.

They flew over the old mill and further down the Zoe River about half a mile, then over the next ridge at the river's bend.

Lacy recognized the little yellow house that lay in the valley below. From here she could also see the intersection with the road called Disobedience that led Soul to a dead end into the Pool of Muck. In the opposite direction, to the north, was the mountain where she first heard the cry of Soul's mother. How beautiful and majestic it looked standing high above the hills. It was as if all of creation was lifting up their hands in that direction, including them. The trees swayed and clapped their hands and the flowers sang in unison a chorus of praise to God. They were joined by other voices; some high, some low, from the rocks, streams and all living things. Even the soft pink, billowing clouds with their wispy voices sang along.

Lacy's desire to fly to the glorious mountain was unwavering, but she felt herself descending. Looking down, she saw Soul's house getting closer. Their feet touched the ground lightly and they were standing at Soul's front door.

Inside they found his mother lying in bed, sick with a high fever. Holy Spirit whispered to Lacy, "Lay your hands upon her head and pray."

"But what am I going to say?" asked Lacy.

"Command that she be healed in Jesus' name," answered Holy Spirit.

So Lacy obeyed, and laid her hands on Grace's head, and Soul did the same.

"Be healed in Jesus' name." Lacy spoke boldly.

Immediately, Soul's mother sat up. She got out of bed and jumped up and down praising the Lord, thanking Him for His great mercy and for sending His angels again.

Then, turning to the pair of angels, she enthusiastically said to Lacy, "Thank you Superfeet, and thank you, uh, Soul, is that you?" "We'll I'll be!"

"It sure is," exclaimed Soul proudly.

"You're welcome," Lacy answered.

"But we didn't do anything. God did it."

"Well, I'm sure grateful you listened to him," said Grace.

"Me too," Soul retorted.

"I didn't get a chance before to thank you for finding Soul and helping him find his way home," said Grace. "I sure appreciate what you did."

"I was glad I could help. It's real nice to see to see you again but I guess I'd better go now," said Lacy. "I'm supposed to be back at the Thompson's before evening."

"The Thompsons? No need to worry, Superfeet. I'll call Vivian." And looking through the window she said, "The sky is getting dark; it looks like it'll rain soon. I think I'd better drive you." Mrs. Young spoke, and so it would be.

The Coming Storm

Grace called Vivian and explained the situation and told her she would be driving Lacy back. The Thompsons invited Grace and Soul to stay for dinner. This made the kids happy, for they were fast becoming good friends.

Grace knew that these were two very special kids. They had somehow learned what adults had not, to obey the Holy Spirit and not limit God's power with disbelief. She marveled at their faith and thought of the scripture that says we must enter the kingdom of God as a child (Mark 10:15 NKJV).

She grabbed a couple of loaves of homemade bread and the blackberry cobbler she had made the day before and handed them to Soul and Lacy.

"Come on, let's go Superfeet," she said.

"You can call me Lacy if you want."

Grace laughed and said, "Of course Lacy, but you are still Superfeet to me."

The three piled into the old truck and headed up the road to the Thompson's. Grace taught them a song that she loved to sing, she explained it was actually a Psalm, and they all sang out loudly and gave God praise, singing, "For thou, Lord, art high above all the earth; thou are exalted far above all gods" (Psalm 97:9 KJV).

Just as the rusty blue truck pulled into the drive, thunder clapped so loud it made them all jump. Huge, dark, swirling clouds moved quickly above, and the wind began to blow violently through the trees overhead. Lacy and Soul were relieved when they pulled up in front of the old house. Mrs. Thompson was standing on the front porch waving everyone inside.

"There's a bad storm rolling in and the sky's growing blacker by the minute," she yelled. "It's about to rain cats and dogs."

The three jumped out of the truck and ran up the steps onto the porch.

As soon as they crested the last step the rain began to pour down.

"Perfect timing," Vivian said to Grace. "Come on in and make yourself at home."

They entered the living room and were greeted by Ben Thompson and Lacy's parents, Frank and Gloria.

"Dinner will be ready in a few minutes," said Vivian. "I hope you're up for pot roast."

"Sounds delicious, I hope this will make a good addition to the meal." said Grace.

Lacy and soul held up the bread and cobbler they were carrying.

"Oh that bread smells so good," said Ben. "And is that a blackberry cobbler under that tea towel?"

Ben lifted up the towel to have a peek.

"Um, um. I'm looking forward to a big piece of that, a la mode."

"Now, now," teased Vivian as she took the pie from Soul, keeping it from Ben.

Spinning around she headed toward the kitchen, Gloria right behind her carrying the bread she had taken from Lacy.

"Nobody makes a better blackberry cobbler than Grace!" exclaimed Ben. "Best little ole pie baker around."

Grace wondered what had gotten into Ben. He's in an unusually good mood.

"Thank you so much," said Grace. "Well, I guess I'd better see if I can help in the kitchen." She left to join Vivian and Gloria.

"Hey Lacy, let's go up and explore the attic and tower while we wait for dinner," said Soul, ready for another adventure.

"Well...," said Lacy slowly. "I don't think we have time right now. Dinner is almost ready."

"How about after dinner?"

"Perhaps," Lacy answered. "But for now I want to show you what I was talking about earlier in Luke 10."

Lacy picked up *The Awesome Book* and she and Soul sat down in the loveseat across the room from Frank and Ben.

Frank watched with fascination as his little girl picked up the big, black book. It was almost as big as her. He chuckled lightly to himself, and noticed Ben also seemed amused. Both men were a little awed by the children's interest in God and the *Awesome Book*. Holy Spirit touched their hearts, but they dismissed it. Soon they were back to discussing the weather and the news.

"What are the disciples, Lacy? Are we disciples?"

"I'm not sure," said Lacy.

"Hey," said Soul. "Let's ask my Mom. I bet she knows. She reads *The Awesome Book* all the time."

Vivian Believes

The call to dinner came and everyone went into the dining room to eat. Vivian's pot roast was delicious, as usual, as was the rest of the meal, including the bread Grace made.

After dinner the men went back into the living room while the women cleaned up the kitchen. Afterward there would be conversation over coffee and cobbler a la mode.

Lacy left the kitchen and returned with *The Awesome Book* that had belonged to her grandpa. She laid the big book on the table and opened it very carefully so she would not tear any pages. She had placed the red shoelace between the pages to mark her place.

"Well, what do we have here?" asked Grace. "That book is about as big as you are," she joked.

"It's *The Awesome Book*. We wanted to ask you what a disciple is. Soul said you would probably know. It says here that his disciples did miracles in Jesus' name."

"And," added Soul "Their names are written in Heaven."

"That's right. A disciple is someone who learns, a pupil, a follower of Jesus," answered Grace.

"Thank you Mrs. Young," said Lacy.

Vivian, who was washing the dishes stopped to listen, and so did Gloria, who was drying.

"What are you reading Lacy?" asked her mother.

"Luke, chapter 10 in *The Awesome Book*," Lacy replied.

Curiosity got the best of Gloria, who hadn't heard much out of *The Awesome Book* since her father had gone to Heaven. Vivian was also interested and they both sat down at the kitchen table to listen as Lacy read the scriptures. The Holy Spirit filled the air and touched everyone's heart, and they knew it was true.

"How do I know if my name's written in Heaven?" asked Vivian.

Grace explained how God sent Jesus to die for our sins, because everyone was guilty of sin and needed a Savior who was pure.

"He was the 'Lamb of God, who takes away the sins of the world' (John 1:29 NKJV). 'If you confess that Jesus is Lord and believe that He was raised from the dead, you shall be saved' (Romans 10:9 NKJV), and your name will be written in the Lamb's Book of Life."

Grace took Vivian's hand and said, "If you would like to know for sure, I will help you. Just tell Jesus in your own words what you believe in your heart and what you want."

Vivian bowed her head and prayed, "Please forgive me Lord, I believe in you. I want my name to be written in heaven, please save me."

Her face became radiant with God's glory and His presence was heavy upon everyone in the room. Lifting their hands to heaven they thanked and gave God praise for his gift of life and for saving Vivian. Even little Todd was affected.

"See, see!" he said, then giggled and kept looking upward curiously. "See!" he said again, and reached his arms up.

Everyone was intrigued by little Todd's reaction and wondered what he was seeing.

"He's so cute," said Grace. She couldn't resist picking him up and giving him a big squeeze.

The two men waiting for their coffee and dessert in the living room had been drawn into the kitchen by Holy Spirit. They were standing in the doorway, looking a bit bewildered.

"What's going on in here?" asked Ben. "Is the coffee and cobbler ready yet?

"I'm sorry," said Gloria. "We'll bring it right out.'

The two men walked back into the living room without saying a word, but both were heavy in thought about what they saw, heard, and felt.

Soon the coffee and cobbler arrived and all was well. Everyone gathered in the living room to have dessert except for Lacy and Soul, who volunteered to sit and eat with little Todd in the kitchen. Milk, ice cream and blackberry cobbler sure hit the spot.

"Can you believe what happened today? Wasn't it a great day Lacy?"

"It sure was a great day!"

"Gateday!" squealed Todd excitedly, over and over, slapping his hands on the highchair.

"Yes, little guy. It was a great day." Lacy said rubbing his head and laughing.

Gloria entered the kitchen to see what the laughter is all about.

"Well, it sounds like everyone's having a good time in here. Incwuding you too wittle Todd." she said in a baby voice.

Then she lifted him up from his high chair.

"My, my, just look at your face."

Todd smiled a wide grin and gave Mom a big hug and kiss, which left a smudge of blackberry cobbler on her cheek.

"I guess I'd better get us both cleaned up," said Gloria with a smile and headed for the bathroom.

"Now what are we going to do?" asked Soul.

"I suppose we could play some games if you like," said Lacy.

"Does Mrs. Thompson have video games that we could play?

"I don't think so," replied Lacy, "just board games. Do you like Scrabble?"

"Not really. I know! We can explore the tower."

"Oh, I really don't want to right now," she said, "maybe some other time."

"But what's wrong with right now? Come on Lacy, it will be fun."

"It's raining and we would have to go outside to get there," she said, crossing her fingers behind her back. *"It was just a little white lie,"* she thought. There was another way through the attic door on the second floor but Rachael and she always used the outside entrance. This explanation seemed to satisfy Soul for now, but Lacy felt a twinge of guilt for fibbing

They settled for Scrabble but soon grew weary of playing.

God's Armor

Soul walked over to the Thompson's kitchen window and pulled back the curtain.

"It's still raining cats and dogs."

Lightning flashed across the entire sky and the sound of thunder shook the house. Though the storm was raging, Lacy could hear the sound of rustling and looked down to see the pages of *The Awesome Book* flipping very quickly. When it stopped, she leaned forward to what Holy Spirit wanted her to read. Her eyes fell on Ephesians, chapter 6, verse 10. She began to read aloud.

"Finally, my brethren, be strong in the Lord and in the power of his might. Put on the whole armour of God, that ye may be able to stand against the wiles of the devil." (Ephesians 6:10-11 KJV).

She continued until she had read through verse 18.

"Wow," said Soul, who was now standing by her listening intently.

"God has armor, and He wants us to put it on? Christopher Curtis and me used to play sword fight when we were little, but we didn't have any armor. How do we get it?"

"Well, it's kinda hard to understand," said Lacy.

Vivian had just walked into the kitchen to fetch more coffee but was drawn into the conversation and sat down.

"My, you two sure talk about some interesting things. Are you sure you're really kids, or aliens in disguise?" she joked.

They all laughed, then Lacy pointed Vivian's attention to verse 10, and she also read through verse 18. Gloria and Grace came in to see if Vivian needed some help and found her sitting at the table with Lacy and Soul reading.

"Grace, Gloria, did you know that God has armor? It says so right here." she said, putting her finger on verse 10. "That's what the kids and I were reading about."

"Yes, I have studied about God's armor," replied Grace. "God knew, against Satan, we were defenseless."

"Hold that thought." said Gloria. "I'll take the men their coffee refills and come right back."

Vivian poured coffee for the ladies and some hot chocolate for the kids. When Gloria returned everyone settled in around the table with their drinks. Grace offered a prayer to the Heavenly Father, in Jesus's name requesting help to understand, and thanking Him for his love and guidance.

As Grace taught from *The Awesome Book*, Holy Spirit shined the light of truth and the words sank deep in their hearts. Lacy and Soul did not realize how soon they would need what they were learning tonight.

"The armor is for our defense in spiritual warfare with God's enemies, and ours." Grace began.

"Jesus has already defeated our enemies through his suffering, death and resurrection. Taking the judgment for our sins, he crushed Satan's power over us. Now we have no reason to fear judgment or the devils accusations and deceptions. We can stand stand strong against the devil and his schemes by clothing ourselves with God's armor."

Grace explained what each piece of armor was, what it was used for, and how Holy Spirit helps us to pray and use God's word like a sword, and about his angels who watch over us and heed God's words. She also explained that not just angels could fight for God, but anyone who believed in the armor and power of God. Grace then taught them about a young boy named David and how God had used him to slay the giant, Goliath, who defied his army.

"I remember the story of David and Goliath," said Gloria. "Dad used to read me those old bible stories. Oh how he loved *The Awesome Book*. He would read from it every morning and night before he went to bed. He always referred to David as a mighty man of valor who loved God with all his heart. I can just picture his face when he talked about him."

Imitating her father Gideon she spoke very dramatically, "David was no stranger to danger. As a shepherd boy he had killed a lion and a bear who took a lamb from his father's flock. (1Samuel 17:34 KJV). He told King Saul that with God's help he would defeat this giant too. From the stream David selected five smooth stones which made them easier to sling. Confident that God was with him he bravely ran toward the giant calling upon the name of the Lord. The first stone was skillfully released from the sling finding its mark and Goliath the giant fell to the ground with a gigantic thud." Her face beamed as she spoke of her father who seemed bigger than life. "Gloria, he would say, "You don't have to be afraid of any giants. Just have faith and tackle everything in the name of Jesus and you'll win."

"He brought down that giant with just one stone?!" asked Soul in astonishment. "I can't wait to tell Chance about David fighting Goliath. He's got a slingshot too!"

Gloria laughed and said, "That's right Soul, just one stone. I guess with God's help that was all he needed." Then she said, "I am really thankful for a father who loved me and taught me about God and his Awesome Book. The last few years I haven't been reading much from it but I'm going to start again. I realize this is what has been missing from my life. I feel like I've come home from from a long journey and found God's welcome arms."

The presence of God filled them all and they rejoiced and praised God for his precious love and The Awesome Book. Then they all held hands and Grace prayed for God to protect the word that was planted in each heart and to clothe them with all his armor and she thanked God for a wonderful time together. They all said a big hearty, "Amen."

Just as they finished their study, Ben came in.

"Well, doesn't look like the storm's gonna let up. One of the trees has been hit by lightning too, and it's covering the drive. Vivian, looks like you'll have to make preparations for everyone to spend the night."

"There's plenty of room," said Vivian with a big smile that defined her squared, but feminine jaw.

"This big, old, empty house could use some company, and so could I!"

Her brown eyes dancing above her high cheekbones, she beckoned them in a silly British accent. "Come ladies, I'll show you to your rooms."

Gloria and Grace laughed and obediently followed after her.

Ben thought to himself, as he watched them climb the stairs chattering and laughing like schoolgirls, that it sure was good to see Vivian happy again. Her short frame almost appeared taller and her chocolate brown hair bounced with her walk, not to mention he'd almost forgotten what a wonderful sense of humor she had.

Soon everyone was settled in snug for the night. Lacy fell back on the bed and thought about the armor of God and everything else that she could remember of what Mrs. Young taught them. *Mrs. Young is so nice* she thought, *and she knows a lot about The Awesome Book.*

Earlier she had overheard Mrs. Thompson tell her mother that Grace was a widow. Thinking of this Lacy suddenly felt a sorrow overwhelm her and she prayed for Soul and Mrs. Young, though she couldn't express it in words. Then she thanked God for her new friends, her parents, the Thompson's and their daughter Rachael. She thanked God for his angels that watched over them all, and asked God to protect Jim too. She praised Jesus's name until she fell asleep, basking in the warmth of God's presence, undisturbed by the thundering outside.

Ben's Revelation

At midnight, Ben Thompson was awakened by a tremendous burst of thunder and he sat straight up in bed quaking. He was relieved it was only thunder and not the voice of God. He remembered reading once that God's voice was like the sound of thunder and every time there's a bad storm he has trouble sleeping.

Getting up, he put on his robe and went to the kitchen to get a drink of water. There on the table before him lay *The Awesome Book*.

"It's just a book," a voice snarled. "Just a book."

Ben turned to see where the ominous voice was coming from but there was no one in the room but him. "Now I'm hearing things," he muttered. "Geesh! Just listen to me. My mind is playing tricks on me and I'm talking to myself. But it is just a book!"

But was it? Ben was struggling all day to explain away the powerful presence that was evident when Vivian was asking God to save her. "Things are getting awfully strange around here," he muttered again.

A loud boom jolted him out of his meditation and a bolt of lightning struck the ground right next to the porch causing the window to rattle. The room grew icy cold and a shiver ran up Ben's spine. Out of thin air a dark cloudy mist appeared above his head for a few moments then vanished. A sense of dread overwhelmed him and he was clearly shaken.

"What if I've been wrong?" he questioned nervously. Maybe it's all real.

He bowed his head and solemnly prayed, "God, I need to know the truth. Is this book really the word of God? Is Jesus the only way?"

When he looked up, *The Awesome Book* was open. *I'm sure it was closed*, he thought. *I'm sure it was!* He scooted his chair in closer to the table and began to read the book of John. He read and read, and he prayed until the dawning light came peeking through the windows. The sense of dread was replaced with peace. He was still sitting at the kitchen table when his wife, Vivian, came in.

"Good morning. You're up early. Is the coffee on?"

"I'm sorry," said Ben. "I hadn't even thought about making coffee."

His dark eyes were worn from reading, but somehow very alive.

"That's okay," replied Vivian. "I'll make a pot. How long have you been up?"

"All night. I couldn't sleep and I was thirsty, so I got up to get a drink of water. I felt troubled so I sat down and prayed God would show me the truth about Jesus. When I looked up, *The Awesome Book* was open and I was drawn to read it." Ben left out the part of the ominous voice and the dark mist.

He looked at Vivian with tears in his eyes and said, "Something wonderful has happened to me. God showed me I need to be born again to enter His Kingdom. I asked him to forgive me and to give me this new birth he was talking about. I wanted Him to save me, like He saved you."

Vivian went over to Ben, and leaning over his broad shoulders, gave him a kiss on the cheek and a big hug.

"What do we do from here?" she asked.

"I don't know," Ben replied. "But I'm going to trust God to show us."

Ben and Vivian moved from the kitchen to the back porch to enjoy their coffee alone. After the rain, the air smelled fresh and clean, just like Ben and Vivian felt. Even though his charcoal hair was greying a little, to Vivian, he looked twenty again. She knew that this was the beginning of an exciting, new adventure for them both. As they were going back inside, Vivian silently thanked God for saving her husband.

Gloria stuck her head in the kitchen and said, "Good morning!"

"Good morning," responded Ben.

"You and little Todd have a seat. Let me get you a fresh, hot cup of coffee and some milk for Todd."

"Why thank you Ben."

"You know," said Vivian. "I had the best sleep I've had in years. I didn't hear a thing once my head hit the pillow."

"Yeah, I know what you mean," said Gloria.

Little Todd let out a squeal of delight and pointed at the door.

"See, see!" he squealed again and again pointing at the door and clapping his hands happily and chuckling.

They looked to see what he was pointing at, but nothing was there except a broom leaning against the wall.

"He sure is a happy child!" exclaimed Vivian.

Soon everyone was gathered in the kitchen and the atmosphere was filled with chatter and laughter, and the smell of bacon frying.

"You know, Ben, nothing smells better than bacon frying," said Frank.

"You'll get no argument outta me Frank. Since I was a child, I can remember waking up to the smell of coffee and bacon."

Breakfast was soon on the table. Ben gave the blessing and everyone dug in. Vivian sure knew how to set a table. She made homemade biscuits, so light they could almost float to heaven, smothered with white gravy. And of course, there was always homemade jam.

"After breakfast," said Ben, "We'll take a look at the damage done by the storm. It may take a while to get that tree cleared from the driveway."

"We had some tremendous winds last night," exclaimed Frank. "I'm surprised you still have electricity. You know, the thunder and lightning kept me up half the night."

"Yeah, me too," said Ben. "It was awfully loud at times."

"Oh no!" cried Soul, suddenly remembering Jim. "We've got to see if Jim's okay."

"Who's Jim?" asked Frank.

"We met Jim when we went exploring yesterday down by the mill. That's where he's living."

"Why didn't you tell us?" asked Grace.

"I kinda forgot," Soul replied.

"Yeah, me too," said Lacy. "We're sorry."

"Are you sure you just forgot Lacy? You surely remember what we have told you about talking to strangers!" said Dad who was clearly upset.

"I know Dad," replied Lacy, "I was afraid to tell you about Jim cause I didn't want to get in trouble, but it turns out he was really a nice guy after all."

"You shouldn't be trying to hide things from us Lacy. You know that was wrong, don't you?" Not waiting for her answer to he added, "And it could have turned out a whole lot different!"

Lacy hung her head and her eyes filled with tears. She couldn't stand for her Dad to be upset with her and her heart ached. "I'm really sorry Daddy. I won't do it again, I promise."

"Frank looked down at Lacy with disappointment and said, "We aren't finished, we'll talk more about this later young lady."

"And you just kinda forgot, did you Soul?" his mother asked.

Soul just stood there with a blank look on his face and couldn't say anything.

"And besides that, You kids need to stay away from that old mill. It's liable to fall in on your heads," warned Mr. Thompson.

"But what about Jim? What if the roof fell in on him?" said Soul with a tearful voice.

"Frank," said Gloria. "Maybe you and Ben should go and check on Jim."

The pleas were too much for the two men and soon they were heading out toward the river, taking the same path as Soul and Lacy. Everyone watched the two from the back porch until they could see them no longer.

"I sure hope Jim is okay," said Soul.

"Me too," Lacy agreed. "Me too."

To The Rescue

The ground was soggy and the path muddy, but Ben and Frank managed to get down the steep hill without falling. When they got close, they could see that a huge tree had fallen in on the mill. Wading through the high weeds, Frank was thankful for the extra pair of high water boots Ben had given him to wear. They were a bit tight, but close enough not to bother him. They made their way around to the front of the mill and found the door wide open, torn from the hinges. Tree branches and rubble was strewn everywhere.

They began to call out Jim's name, asking if he was okay.

"I'm over here," a voice called back. The tree filled the room, but the men were able to reach Jim without much difficulty. The problem would be getting him out. He was under a broken table, beneath a huge branch and couldn't move. Luckily, the tree's weight was supported by the remaining wall.

"Are you all right?" asked Ben.

"I will be as soon as I get out of here," grunted Jim. "I'm feeling a bit squashed."

Ben looked at Frank, "Do you mind staying here with Jim while I go back and get a chainsaw?"

"No need for that," groaned Jim again, his tight, light brown curls hanging in his eyes, blocking half of his view. "I've got one in the back of my truck, if it survived. And gas if you need it."

Ben went to retrieve the chainsaw and returned with it in hand. It wasn't long until Jim was free.

"I sure appreciate you guys helping me out," said Jim. "How did you know I was here?"

"Soul and Lacy told us. I'm Frank, Lacy's father, and this is Ben Thompson," said Frank. "The kids didn't bother mentioning you until this morning and that was only because they were worried about you and fessed up. Needless to say, I wasn't too happy about them hangin out with a total stranger."

"Well you can't be too careful these days," said Jim, "can't say as I blame you. I was trying to run them off at first, but I guess God had other things in mind. Man, that's two times now they've helped me out. I was wondering how I was going to get out of that predicament, so I sure was glad to see you guys." After he put the chainsaw back in the truck bed he said, "Thanks for listening to those kids," and he stuck out his hand to shake theirs. "It's sure nice to meet you both." Ben returned the gesture and Frank too. It began to rain lightly again, so the three men crowded into the beat-up pickup.

Frank and Ben listened as Jim told them about what had happened when he met the kids the day before. Frank and Ben seemed pretty amazed when Jim told them that God told Lacy his name. They just gave each other a funny look. When he got to the part about Jenny being happy he was saved, he began to cry.

"I finally knew what she was trying to tell me all them years."

Ben put his hand on Jim's shoulder, "I'm sorry about your wife," he said. "I can't imagine what I would do without my Vivian. She and my daughter Rachael are my whole life."

Frank also felt a pain in his heart and a big lump came up in his throat. He could almost feel Jim's pain, and he prayed silently for him. For once, he was at a loss for words.

"Hey Jim," sad Ben, "Why don't you come back to the house with us for some dry clothes and some hot coffee. I bet you could use a good breakfast too."

"I don't want to be any inconvenience to you and your wife, Ben. I appreciate what you and Frank have already done."

"Now Jim," Frank chimed in. "Those kids are sure worried about you. I know they would like to see that you are safe and sound. I think maybe I was a little hard on Lacy about talking to you. I'm feeling a little bad about it now," he admitted. "I didn't realize the circumstances. I'd like for you to come also."

Jim grinned, "I'd sure like to see them young-uns again too. All right, if I can just get this old truck started, we'll be on our way. It usually takes a little coaxing, especially in wet weather."

Jim turned the key and the run down truck started on the first try. *Strange* he thought, and then said, "Point the way," as he pulled onto Old Mill Road.

It wasn't long until they pulled into the Thompson's driveway, but they didn't get much farther than the entrance.

"Looks like we'll have to walk the rest of the way," said Jim. "I'll help you get those fallen trees out of the driveway if you like."

"I'll take you up on that later," Ben replied getting out of the truck. "Right now, I could use a hot cup of coffee and some dry clothes. I'll fix you guys up with some clothes too; they should fit well enough."

Lacy and Soul were waiting when the men came in front of the door and were relieved to see Jim. Vivian insisted that Jim have a hot breakfast and went right to work despite Jim saying she didn't have to go to no trouble.

Soon Jim was looking wide eyed at a plate full of biscuits, gravy, bacon, eggs, and a jar of homemade jam; Topped off with a cup of piping hot coffee.

"Boy, that sure looks good," He said.

"You think it looks good, just wait until you taste it," said Ben.

"My Viv is a fine cook," he bragged and pulled her close to his side.

Jim hardly came up for air between bites. Each bite was followed by an "um" or a, "boy that's good."

He had to agree with Ben that Vivian was a mighty fine cook.

Grace was sitting on the back porch reading from *The Awesome Book* when the men returned. She came back in the kitchen door just as Jim finished eating.

"Jim," said Ben. "This is our friend, and Soul's mother, Grace."

"Hello," said Grace sheepishly, her brown eyes just as familiar as Soul's, met his and she reached out her hand to shake his.

"Hello," replied Jim, nervously taking Grace's hand. "It's very nice to meet you. You sure have a fine son, a fine boy that Soul."

"Thank you," expressed Grace whose timidity was replaced with a proud smile.

Gloria and Frank looked at each other and winked.

"More coffee anyone," said Vivian, holding up the coffee pot. "I've got a fresh pot right here."

She filled Jim's cup again and set a cup for Grace next to him.

The Mystery of the Tower

Now that he knew Jim was safe, Soul wanted to explore the attic and tower. The tower and the attic were on opposite sides of the top landing of the servant's staircase. Even though the tower was much smaller than the attic, it was still a fun place to play. Rachael Thompson used them both for playrooms when she was a girl. It was she who dubbed it *"The Tower."*

"Come on," whined Soul. "It'll be an adventure."

"Yeah, a scary one," Lacy whined back. I'm not going!

"But you said that you would, and I don't want to go by myself."

"How come? Are you scared?" Lacy taunted.

"You're the one that's scared! Not me! It's just that you said you would. Now you're backing out!"

"I said maybe after dinner!" replied Lacy curtly, "and that was last night."

Soul dropped his head, and without a word turned and walked away. Suddenly Lacy felt bad about how she had talked to Soul and called out for him to come back.

I'm Sorry," she said. "It's just that the last time I was up there I saw something that looked like a dark shadow and it moved toward me and then it looked like it was standing right over me. It was Creepy!"

"Didn't you tell anyone about it," asked Soul?

"No, I didn't."

Just the thought made her shudder.

But knowing Soul's curiosity would not be satisfied until she showed him, reluctantly, she gave in.

"Okay, Come on. We'll go outside and up through the servants entrance."

Soul had finally won and was anxious to go. "All right! Led the way Superfeet!"

The old spiraled stairway creaked with every step, which only increased the feeling of eeriness. Lacy's heart was thumping so loudly she was sure that Soul could hear it.

They had passed the second floor landing and had finally reached the top of the staircase. They were standing on the top of the landing looking around the small area that led to the attic and the tower, Lacy asked, "Where to first?"

"Where did you see the shadow?" Soul questioned back.

"In there." Lacy pointed to the doorway on the left that lead into the tower room.

"Well…" Soul motioned toward the door.

Lacy reached for the door, as she pushed it open slowly it made a spooky sound. Screeeeeech!

"Boo!" yelled Soul.

Lacy screamed and almost came out of her shoes.

"Stop that Soul!" Lacy spouted. "That's not funny!"

Soul, however, found Lacy's response amusing and laughed.

"Okay then, you can go in first." said Lacy, a bit irritated.

Lacy stepped into the room behind

Soul and stuck close to his heels as he walked over to the main window. The room was small, but Soul thought it was a perfect place to hang out.

"This is the coolest!" he exclaimed. "From here we can see the path to the river and a bit of the valley beyond the grove of trees."

"Yeah, I know," said Lacy feeling very uncomfortable, her eyes searching the room.

Soul turned back toward Lacy and looked around the room eyes scanning every nook and cranny.

"See, there's nothing here," he said with a sly grin. "It was probably just your imagination."

"I know what I saw," she pouted back. "It was not just my imagination."

Seeing that he had irritated her, Soul tried to smooth it over by saying "Maybe it was a shadow from a tree outside that was moving and it just looked like it was standing over you."

He no sooner spoke than a chill filled the air causing them to shiver, and then suddenly out of nowhere a dark shadow darted in front of them so close they felt it brush their clothes.

"Did you see that?" asked Soul nervously, his eyes wide.

Now Lacy had Soul's attention.

"I told you it was real. Let's get out of here!" said Lacy fearfully as she headed for the door.

A ghastly face appeared with a hideous smile blocking the way and it spoke hauntingly, snarling, "Where do you think you're going?"

They shuddered with fear and wanted to scream but couldn't. The dark thing came back at them again and forcefully shoved Lacy, causing her to groan and fall back against Soul. He stumbled beneath her, but managed to lift her back on her feet and they both headed for the door again. Just as they reached it, the door slammed shut with a jarring thud. Frantically, Soul jerked on the door knob, but it fell off in his hand.

"We're trapped." cried Soul in distress. "What are we going to do?

The shadowy phantom mocked Soul, "We're trapped! What are we going to do…?" and laughed fiendishly, "aah…, ha, ha, ha, ha…," then he pounced on them again, this time knocking them both off their feet.

"Jesus!" cried Lacy. "Help!"

Lacy felt the power of God rise up in her and she cried out, "Be strong in the Lord and in the power of His might! Stand up in Jesus's name and fight!"

Instantly Soul and Lacy sprang to their feet shouting, "We come at you in the name of the Lord Jesus, the Christ."

Swoosh, their words cut through the air and the hideous dark shadow was hurled backward.

They watched in astonishment as the room filled with God's light. They were now dressed in white tunics with a wide gold belt around their waists. Attached to it was a breastplate of pure gold and a gold scabbard for the swords of light they were holding high. Soul had on brilliant blue trousers. Upon their heads sat a gold helmet, and on their feet, red boots with red shoelaces. In their left hand they both held a large golden shield that deflected the fiery arrows the wicked one was shooting at them. The arrows appeared out of thin air, hit their shields and fell to the floor in front of them and vanished.

"The armor of God!" shouted Soul. "We've got on the armor of God!"

"Leave this house in Jesus name!" Lacy commanded through the power of Holy Spirit.

Soul repeated the command using his authority with great power also.

Swoosh, their swords found its mark and the dark form shrieked in terror.

Then Lacy prayed, *thank you Lord for your angels which have charge over us*. And right before their eyes appeared a large golden haired angel clothed with light, wearing gold armor too, and holding a great sword. Written in silver across his breastplate was the name Jared. He was so tall that his helmet went through the ceiling. Then appeared another angel clothed in light and armor with the name Ashkea on the breastplate, also written in silver. This one had dark brown hair and large hazel colored eyes. The angel moved quickly between the hideous dark shadow and Lacy and Soul, and stood with sword in hand. The dark figure again screamed in horror, this time in a high pitched, agonizing wail. Desperately trying to escape, it went right through the tower door, but the angel Jared reached his hand through the door and grabbed that evil spirit by the throat, pulling him back through. All the while the dark thing was struggling frantically to free itself.

"The large angel bent down and with his bright blue eyes looked at Lacy and Soul dressed in Jesus's armor and smiled, then gave a wink. He then turned and looked angrily at the evil spirit he had caught, hurled the dark figure through the wall of the house with a great force, and then he followed. The second angel turned and smiled at the young warriors with the softest and kindest eyes that Lacy thought she had ever seen, and then suddenly vanished.

"Wow, Lacy. Wasn't that the coolest thing you ever saw? That was one big angel. No wonder the evil spirit was scared! There's no one stronger than God and his angels. At first I was the one who was really scared. That spirit was really mean!"

"Yeah, I sure know what you're saying," replied Lacy. "I was really frightened too at first. But it was just like *The Awesome Book* said. God gave us his armor and sword to fight with and sent his angels. I've never seen an angel before. They sure were awesome, weren't they? And beautiful!"

"They sure were! Oh, man that was so…awesome! Then Soul hung his head and said, "By the way I'm really sorry I didn't believe you."

"That's okay, Soul, I understand. I'm sorry too, for the way I acted and for fibbing to you about not being able to explore the tower. There is another entrance into the attic; a door to a stairway on the second floor."

"Well, I can see now why you didn't want to come up here, but I'm real glad you did. Friends?" asked Soul.

"Friends," said Lacy with a big smile.

Though they could no longer see the armor, they could feel the power of the Holy Spirit still upon them. They were a bit stunned but excited about everything that had just happened; there was a deeper sense of awe and love for God. They lifted their arms up to Heaven and began to sing the song that Soul's mother taught them.

"For thou, Lord, art high above all the earth; though art exalted far above all Gods." (Psalm 97:9 KJV).

Lacy and Soul's faces were glowing when they finally came down from the top landing. As they descended the creaky stairway, Lacy turned to Soul and said, "We'll be going home as soon as the driveway is cleared. That's what Dad told Mom this morning. We really had some great adventures Soul, just like Jesus's disciples. I hope we get to have some more."

"Sure Superfeet," replied Soul with a big grin.

Lacy just laughed and said, "Come on."

When the two warriors returned to the kitchen, it was just in time for lunch.

"I thought I was gonna have to come and look for you two," said Grace as she studied their faces. "What have you been up to?"

Glancing over at Lacy and smiling, Soul said, "Oh, just exploring the tower and solving its mysteries."

"Soul wanted Lacy to show him the tower, as the kids call it, and I told him it would be all right," said Vivian. "For some reason kids find the mystery of the old tower just too hard to resist."

"Well I can see that," said Frank, who had just come in with Ben and Jim from outside. "I always liked a good adventure. I did some exploring and solved a few mysteries myself when I was that age." He added, "Vivian now that the drive is clear, we'll be getting out of your hair."

"Oh, I've enjoyed every minute of your and Gloria's company, Frank, and I know Ben has too. Now I insist you have some lunch before you go. I made enough to feed an army."

"I was hoping you would say that," said Frank, his blue eyes lighting up. "All that work has made me awfully hungry."

He poured himself some coffee and sat down at the kitchen table beside Gloria who was holding little Todd on her lap. She looked so beautiful today with her strawberry blonde hair cascading around her face. Her almond shaped eyes, that matched Lacy's exactly, were smiling at him extra bright this morning also.

Everyone gathered around the table and enjoyed Vivian's homemade chicken and dumplings and one of the leftover loaves of homemade bread that Grace had brought. And of course, there was always jam.

"Mm, um, um," mumbled Jim after taking his first bite and every other one after.

"Jim," said Soul, "My mom can cook real good too, can't you Mom?"

Soul's intentions could not be mistaken, so Grace gave in, "Maybe you would like to come for dinner some time?" She shyly asked twisting a lock of her short, blond hair that framed her round face.

"You just tell me when," said Jim. "I'll be there fork in hand."

"That won't be necessary," chuckled Grace.

Frank and Gloria looked at each other and winked again. Ben picked up Vivian's hand and gave it a loving squeeze.

Lacy and Soul finally got their chance to tell everyone about the incident in the tower. They were all astounded at what the two were saying, and wondered if it could really be true, but in their hearts, they knew it was, especially Ben.

"I knew there was something upstairs somewhere," said Vivian. "I had been hearing noises lately. Well, I guess I don't have to worry about that now, thanks to you kids."

"And to God for sending His angels," said Lacy with an ear to ear grin.

Little Todd's eyes widened, glistening just like his dads and he pointed at the two angels standing by the kitchen door and chuckled. Clapping his hands he said loudly, "See, see!"

Everyone looked, but saw nothing except the broom leaning against the wall. Everyone that is, but Lacy, Soul and Little Todd.

Grandpa's Treasure

After a big yawn, Lacy sat up and turned on the lamp on the table next to her bed. After rubbing the sleep from her eyes, she got up to take a peek from her bedroom window. Day was just beginning to dawn, and she could only see the silhouettes of the birch trees near the end of the driveway. She raised the window and leaned out to take a big whiff of the crisp morning air.

"It will be daylight soon," she whispered, and sat down on the side of her bed.

Lacy glanced down at her most precious possession. Her thoughts turned to Grandpa and she reached over and gently stroked the red shoelace placed between the pages for a bookmark. She loved Grandpa and missed the wonderful walks and talks they enjoyed together. She remembered how he often spoke of the precious treasures *The Awesome Book* contained, and how he would sit and read to her even as a small child. He never tired of repeating its wonderful stories and he told them with such passion. As

Lacy thought of the riches Grandpa said she would surely find, a joy filled her heart and she let out a squeal of delight. Pressing her finger to her lips, she hushed herself.

Very carefully, Lacy picked up the big, black book with the "powerful words," as Grandpa had called them. She opened the book to where the red shoelace lay and her eyes fell on the words that Grandpa had underlined with a red pen. "I love them that love me; and those that seek me early shall find me." (Proverbs 8:17 KJV).

Lacy closed her eyes and prayed, "God, I got up especially early today to find your wisdom like *The Awesome Book* says. Grandpa says we have to obey what the powerful words speak."

Suddenly, rushing wind blew through the open window causing the curtains to flutter wildly. Lacy felt the wind whirling all around her and wanted to look, but was afraid to. Finally she dared to sneak a peek and then, opening her eyes wide, she beheld a glorious sight. Light was dancing through the wind illuminating every corner of the room with dazzling prisms of light. Lacy was speechless in awesome wonderment until she heard his voice softly saying, "I've been waiting for you to come, Lacy. I love you very much."

"Wow," said Lacy, "You do? It's just like Grandpa said?"

"Yes, dear Lacy, and just like Grandpa told you, I knew you and loved you before you were born."

"How?" she questioned.

He laughed and said, "Lacy, I know all about you because I created you. I have a special plan for your life. That is what I have shown you. I declare the end from the beginning." (Isaiah 46:10 KJV).

"Oh Lord!" Lacy exclaimed, "Is this the treasure Grandpa told me about?"

"Yes, Lacy. If you follow me, you will find treasure worth more than gold."

"Oh Lord, that sounds so wonderful, but where are we going?"

"To the land of All," he replied.

"How do we get there?" asked Lacy.

"Through me, the Son of God, *I* am the way."

But I thought I was going to meet God, she thought to herself, a bit disappointed.

"I would be delighted to introduce you. It is required that you come to God through me," the Lord said, answering Lacy's thoughts.

"Do you trust the words of The Awesome Book dear child?"

"Sure I do! Grandpa says that the words are true and have power!"

The wind encompassed her again and the voice called out as the wind departed through the window, "Read John, chapter 14."

She was feeling exhilarated from the presence of the wind and chuckled to herself.

"Thank you, I will. I will."

With great expectation, Lacy paged through the big, black book until the bold lettering of "The Gospel of John" appeared. Her heart almost leapt out of her chest.

"I found it! Grandpa said gospel means 'good news.' I will surely find fortune here."

She lightly traced over each word with her finger as she softly read again, "The Gospel of John."

After reading verses 1 through 7 Lacy stopped. Her mind could clearly picture Grandpa reading from The Awesome Book, "For God so loved the world that he gave his only begotten Son, that whosoever believeth in him should not perish, but have everlasting life." (John 3:16 KJV).

"Little Lacy," he would say, "One day you will understand that Jesus died for your sins. But also know this, that he rose from the dead and is alive, and he has the power to give everlasting life."

"Oh Jesus," she cried out, "Please forgive me, I believe in you. I believe in you!"

Jesus spoke tenderly to her heart, "I forgive you."

Lacy continued to read until she finished the chapter, then laid aside the book and prayed again, "Jesus, will you come and live in me and bring your Father and Holy Spirit like the powerful words say?"

"I have been waiting for you to ask," answered Jesus.

Lacy looked down from the lofty white clouds and took a deep breath and sighed.

"I so love it up here. I could stay forever."

Leaning back on her elbows she swung her feet back and fourth and admired her beautiful red boots and her shining white tunic which appeared iridescent in the Glory Light.

"One day I will come again on clouds of glory and you will see me face to face," said Jesus.

"Oh, how wonderful that will be Lord Jesus! How wonderful that would be Father!"

"Yes, my child, wonderful," said Heavenly Father, "Yes, absolutely wonderful," whispered Holy Spirit.

Lacy looked down at Grandpa's treasure beside her, picked it up and pressed it to her heart. Hugging it tightly she exclaimed, "Wow Grandpa! This really is *The Most Awesome Book* ever!"

Afterword

"How beautiful upon the mountains are the feet of him that brings good news, who proclaims peace; who brings tidings of good things, who proclaims salvation; who says to Zion, your God reigns!" (Isaiah 52:7 NKJV)